Published by, Zara Mason Publishing
ISBN: 978-1-7398551-4-7

Author, Lucy Minas
Designed by, Angela Price

Contributor, Becky Frewin, MSc, CertMRCSLT, HCPCreg, MASLTIP
Speech & Language Therapist
www.beckyfrewin.com

Follow Ralph online; instagram.com/readwithralph
facebook.com/readwithralph

All rights reserved. This book, or any portion thereof,
may not be reproduced or used in any manner whatsoever without
express prior written permission of the copyright owner.

The rights of Lucy Minas to be identified as the author
and owner of this work has been asserted in accordance
with the Copyright, Designs and Patents Act 1988.

Ralph and the
Red Ribbon Riddle

This book is dedicated to Ralph,
the kindest Great Dane you could ever wish to meet.

Today it is Ralph's birthday,
but he is feeling rotten.
His friends are nowhere to be seen,
have they all forgotten?

'Ralph!' called Roxie Robin, 'look over by the trees.'
A pretty bright red ribbon was flapping in the breeze.

Ralph rapidly ran over, through the rough long grass,
and some cheeky rowdy rabbits cheered as he hurried past.
'Who has left this bright red ribbon?' Ralph just didn't know,
as he looked a little closer, a written riddle began to show.

We didn't forget your birthday,
run to the river for your next clue.
Look for Ricky Rat and he'll show
you what to do!

'I love an adventure,' Ralph replied,
and he started to relax.
Feeling refreshed, he quickly set off,
and followed the river tracks.

Ricky Rat was ready, he knew Ralph was on his way.
He hoped Ralph didn't realise, the plans for later that day.

Ralph ran over to Ricky, 'hello Ralph, how are you?
Are you ready and excited for your next red ribbon clue?'

We didn't forget your birthday,
run to the warren for your next clue.
Call for Ruby Rabbit and she'll show
you what to do!

Ruby Rabbit was rolling around, nibbling on raspberries and roots. 'Ritzy rockets, who goes there? Are you trying to steal my fruits?'

'No Ruby Rabbit, I've come to search out my next clue.'
'Oh!', roared Ruby, 'here it is, be gone now, shoo, shoo, shoo!'

we didn't forget your birthday,
run to the pen for your next clue.
Seek out Rory Ram and he'll show
you what to do!

Ralph started to feel ravenous, his poor belly began to rumble.
Then it started to rain, he got fed up and his thoughts became all jumbled.
What a rotten rubbish birthday, ruined beyond repair.
Did anyone remember Ralph's birthday, did anyone even care?

Ralph retired under a tree, as the raindrops rattled and rolled.
Resting and reflecting, wondering how this day would unfold.

Receiving a birthday treat would be nice, a cake with raspberry jam, and suddenly he remembered, his meeting with Rory the Ram!

Ralph reluctantly ran, through the dreary rain,
Rory Ram was waiting, but Ralph said, 'not again!'
Ralph respectfully continued, 'please not another clue,
I'm feeling rather hungry and don't know what to do!'

Your birthday treat is nearly here, please don't stop now.
There is only one more clue to find, and it's with Christy Cow!

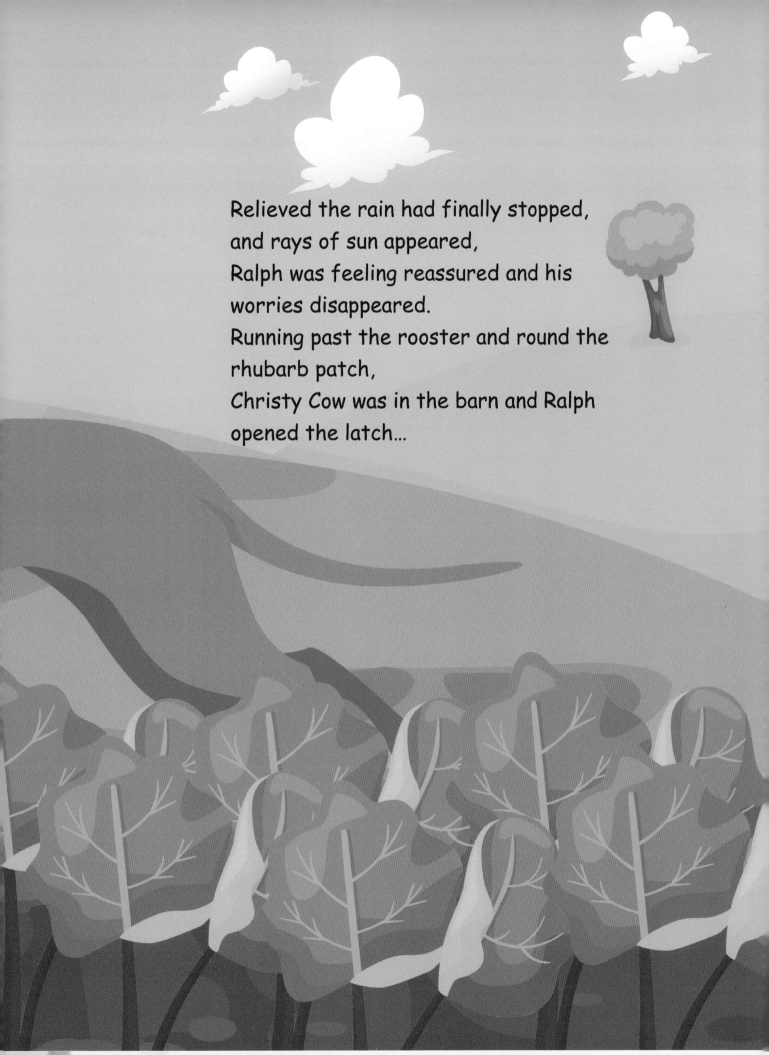

Relieved the rain had finally stopped,
and rays of sun appeared,
Ralph was feeling reassured and his
worries disappeared.
Running past the rooster and round the
rhubarb patch,
Christy Cow was in the barn and Ralph
opened the latch...

Ralph could hear loud rumbles of rushing hooves and paws.
All Ralph's friends revealed themselves giving rapturous applause!
'Hooray for Ralph!' they cheered, 'he's rather remarkable and clever.
We wanted to really surprise you, and give you the best birthday ever!'

The animals all rallied round, a ritzy party Ralph did see,
he was so relieved and said aloud, 'you did all this for me?'

Roxie Robin flew next to Ralph, 'it's your birthday, relax and have fun.' Ralph loved his red ribbon adventure, 'thank you everyone!'

Ralph looked up at all the trees,
rainbow ribbons everywhere.
His friends were truly amazing at
showing they really care.
Rory, Ruby, Ricky and Roxie had
one last surprise,
a raspberry rainbow cream cake,
Ralph couldn't believe his eyes!

R r

Ralph is a very clever dog, finding all of the clues for his birthday surprise! Ralph's name begins with the sound 'r' which can be a very difficult sound to make. If you are finding it tricky, practise these handy tips to help you.

'O' SHAPE

When you're making the 'r' sound, make sure your lips are round, pretend to be a fish and make your lips into a round 'O' shape, this is the shape you need to make a 'r' sound.

You'll also need to move your tongue! The sides of your tongue need to touch the top molar teeth. If you're having trouble finding where to put your tongue, ask an adult to put some jam, chocolate spread, or other yummy treat on them, your tongue will soon find its way. But what about the front of your tongue? When the sides of your tongue know where they are going, just bunch or scrunch up the front of your tongue.

VERY IMPORTANT VOWELS!

The 'r' sound is often easier if you put it between 2 vowels. If you find these hard, start with ooroo, your lips stay round for the whole sound, so it should be the easiest to get started with!

Try saying some of these sounds:

ahrah   eeree
owrow   ohroh
ooroo

Raspberry

Rabbit

Robin

WORD SEARCH

Try finding some words in the story that begin with the 'r' sound – I can think of Ralph, red, rabbit and raspberry. Can you think of any more? Do any words have 'r' in the middle of the word? Are these easier to say? Have a go!

When you can say these words on their own, try putting them in a sentence – these are good ways to start:

I see..
I have found..
I like..

Rat

Ram

FINALLY ...

Remember that 'r' is one of the trickiest sounds to say! You may need some help from a speech and language therapist like me! We are people who help children and grown ups with their speaking, listening and communication. We would be happy to give you some extra tips and tricks if you're finding the 'r' sound difficult.

Have fun practising   Love Becky

Printed in Great Britain
by Amazon

70214031R00017